The Wind
Is Not a River

The Wind Is Not a River

Arnold A. Griese

illustrated by Glo Coalson

Boyds Mills Press

Text copyright © 1978 by Arnold A. Griese
Illustrations copyright © 1996 by Glo Coalson

Published by Caroline House
Boyds Mills Press, Inc.
A Highlights Company
815 Church Street
Honesdale, Pennsylvania 18431
Printed in the United States of America

Publisher Cataloging-in-Publication Data
Griese, Arnold A.
    The wind is not a river / by Arnold A. Griese ; illustrated by Glo Coalson.
[128]p. : ill. ; cm.
Originally published by Thomas Y. Crowell, N.Y., 1978.
Summary : Set during the second World War two children discover a wounded
Japanese soldier on the beach of their small island off the coast of Alaska.
ISBN 1-56397-564-5
1. World War, 1939-1945—Campaigns—Alaska—Aleutian Islands—Juvenile fic-
tion. 2. Aleutian Islands (Alaska)—Juvenile fiction. [1. World War, 1939-1945—
Campaigns—Alaska—Aleutian Islands—Fiction. 2. Aleutian Islands
(Alaska)—Fiction.] I. Coalson, Glo, ill. II. Title.
813.54—dc20   [F]   1996   AC
Library of Congress Catalog Card Number 95-78288

First Boyds Mills Press edition, 1996
The text of this book is set in 12-point New Baskerville
The illustrations are done in watercolor washes

10 9 8 7 6 5 4 3

To Periscovia Wright, who was living on Attu
on that Sunday morning it was captured,
and
To Kathleen Blakely, my newest granddaughter

CONTENTS

About This Story ix

Sad Saturday 1

The Visitors 15

The Village Is Taken 26

Living Off the Land 39

The Night Visit 56

A New Problem 68

The Soldier 81

The Third Night 95

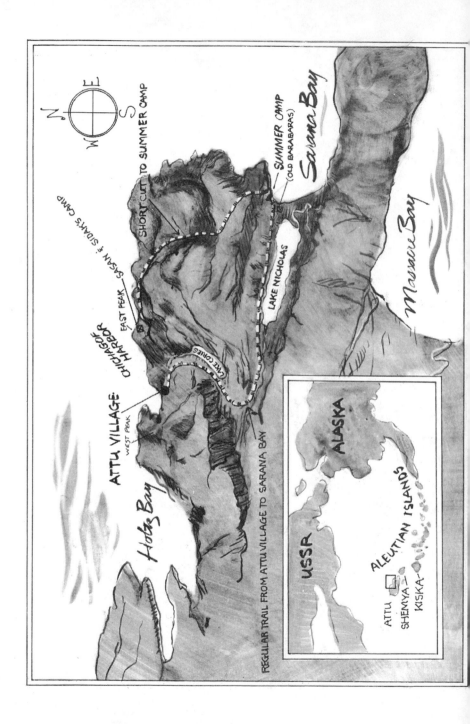

ABOUT THIS STORY

On December 7th, 1941, Japanese planes attacked Pearl Harbor and the people of the United States found themselves in World War II. This war changed the lives of most people. But on the tiny Alaskan island of Attu far out in the Pacific Ocean, and very close to Japan itself, the forty-seven Aleuts living in their village in Chichagof Harbor knew little about this war. Ships came to the island only once or twice each year. There was only one radio on the island. It was in the new school-house and not always able to reach out the thousands of miles to the Alaska mainland.

The war was brought closer to the people of Attu when the school radio brought news of the bombing of Dutch Harbor on the nearby island of Unalaska by Japanese planes on June 3rd, 1942. Then on Sunday morning June 8th, 1942 trouble came to Attu. Early on that still morning Japanese soldiers landed at Holtz Bay, across the mountain from Attu Village. They planned to capture the village while the people were still sleeping. But the island was covered by a thick blanket of fog and the soldiers lost their way in the mountain passes. Meanwhile, the people of Attu, not knowing that enemy soldiers were already on their island, began their Sunday morning as they always did by getting up and going to church.

It was not until noon that the Japanese soldiers finally arrived at the village. Church was over and all was quiet when the first shots rang out. People hurried out of their homes to find enemy soldiers on all sides of them. The war had come to their tiny village.

The story in this book is about the people of Attu and their time of trouble. The island and its people were indeed captured by Japanese soldiers during World War II. However, it is a story, and does not tell everything just as it actually happened. But maybe, by reading about the adventures of Sasan and her brother, you will come to know the courage of the Aleut people as they face the dangers of war.

SAD SATURDAY

On the first Saturday in June, in the year 1942, the wind and the waters from the sea threw themselves against the shores and steep mountains of Attu Island. But in a sheltered harbor, Sasan felt only a cold breeze against her face as she stood next to her younger brother, Sidak. The rest of the people of this tiny Aleutian village were gathered close behind them.

For a moment the sun broke through the low moving clouds. Bright sunshine fell on the gleaming white church nearby and on the uncovered heads of the villagers. Sasan did not see any of this. Her eyes were on a freshly dug hole and the plain wooden box that rested inside.

Tears streamed down her cheeks as she remembered her grandmother's last words: "Sasan, do not be sad. I am not afraid. I have had a long life; and I have had my share of happy times. Now you must promise me you will keep the Old Ways and will make Sidak keep them too."

The sharp cry of a raven floated across from the other side of the village, near the school, breaking Sasan's thoughts. Slowly she bent over and took up a handful of black earth. She squeezed it and felt its coldness flow into her hand. Then she opened her fingers and gently tossed the warmed earth onto the box.

A moment later a strong hand touched her shoulder and she felt herself being led down the green hillside towards her house. The sun shone warm on Sasan's short black hair. But she felt only the cold sadness in her heart.

Towards evening of that same day Sasan sat at the kitchen table. Sidak sat across from her nibbling at some cooked fish. One of the village mothers who would be staying overnight with them had brought them food before leaving to prepare supper for her own family.

All was quiet until at last Sasan asked, "Why is Father not here now? He should be here helping us keep the Old Ways as Grandmother wants us to."

Sidak was looking out the window and did not answer. His eyes followed a small boat moving from the sea into the harbor. Its new outboard motor made it go faster than the bidarki which Grandmother had built for Sasan and him to use.

Sasan saw he was not listening, but she said nothing. She looked down at the long sleeves of her dress which covered her slender brown arms. Just before he left the island, Father had taken her to the village store and had bought this dress and another one and also a pair of walking shoes she liked. Grandmother had always let her wear them. Over a year had passed since her mother died. But Sasan remembered well that terrible time. Tears filled her eyes as she remembered how after that her father and grandmother had quarreled over the Old Ways.

Sidak looked away from the window and saw her tears. Sasan wiped them quickly away with her sleeve. He said, "Father is not wrong. He believed the new medicine could have kept Mother from dying." He stopped for a moment and Sasan heard anger in his voice when he went on, "Father is not against the Old Ways. But he knows we can learn new things. He left our island so he can learn some of these things."

Sidak was not yet ten years old. Sasan knew how much he loved his father and how much he missed him. She was sorry for the words she had just spoken. "You are right," she said. "Father does believe in the Old Ways. That is why he wanted us to live with Grandmother."

She waited for her brother to speak. When he did not, she added, "When he hears that Grandmother has died, he will come back to stay." Sasan missed him, too, and hoped with all her heart that he would come back soon and never leave again.

For a long while they looked out the kitchen window and said nothing. From where Sasan sat she could see the quiet waters of the harbor and the waves dashing against the rocks that kept the angry sea out. She saw boats pulled up on the beach and village men working on them. A small boy ran out of one of the houses that stood along the beach. He hurried down to where his father was mending a fishing net.

"If only Father were here," Sasan thought, "then Sidak would be down at the beach now helping him get ready for the move to summer fishing camp." Restlessness grew inside her as she looked over at their bidarki lying on the beach in among the other boats.

The old clock in the front room chimed six times and Sasan got up with a start. She began clearing the table. As she worked, an idea came to her. "Sidak," she said, "we cannot just sit here doing nothing. Why don't we leave for camp tonight instead of waiting until Monday?"

Sidak's face brightened. "I'll go tell Chief Joseph we're going. You get the things ready, and I'll help carry them down to the bidarki," he said.

The sun had set and low clouds covered the tops of both East and West Peaks by the time their slender skin-covered boat was loaded and ready to go. Sasan sat in the back hole and used her paddle to point the sleek bow towards the harbor opening. Sidak sat straight and tall in the front hole, happy to be on his way. In a moment his paddle and Sasan's were dipping from side to side as if they were one, and the tiny boat skimmed across the quiet harbor.

When they passed out into the open sea, the boat

bobbed and danced over the swells and the choppy waves. But it was always under the control of Sasan's paddle as she headed it around the sharp cliffs of East Peak. Past these cliffs lay Sarana Bay and their summer camp. Here on the open water a cold wind was blowing, and up ahead Sasan saw a heavy rain shower moving across their path toward the shore. Now she was glad they were wearing their raincoats, those light oilskin jackets their grandmother had always called by the old name—kamleika. She stopped paddling long enough to tighten and tie the drawstrings on both sleeves and the one on her hood so the rain could not get in. Then she took up her paddle again and called to her brother, "Tie your raincoat. There is a heavy rain shower ahead."

Sidak turned his head and grinned. Then he laid his paddle carefully in its holder and did as he was told. Sasan felt a special tenderness as she watched him carefully check the drawstring that held the bottom of the raincoat over the bidarki hole so that no water could spill in during the storm. She was only three years older than Sidak but here, far from land and with the wind starting to blow stronger, he seemed all at once so much smaller.

When he had finished checking, he turned back

and grinned again before picking up his paddle. His easy grin told her that he was happy to be out here with her in this small boat, that he trusted her.

It would take over an hour more of paddling to reach their camp at Sarana Bay. That did not worry Sasan. It would not get dark until midnight and that was still hours away. Something else was worrying her now. The heavy rain shower she had spotted earlier had now spread out and had turned much darker. Around its edges, wispy layers of clouds hung down and were being driven along by a strong wind.

For a moment Sasan thought of turning around, but it was already too late. The rain shower was now a real storm. Although it was still moving toward shore, it was also coming her way. Within minutes the wind picked up speed and flung salty spray in her face. Then suddenly, it shifted slightly to the left. Sasan felt the bow of the boat swing to the right as if shoved by an unseen hand. She yelled to her brother, "Keep your paddle on the side opposite the wind. That will keep us from being blown around."

Sidak swung his paddle over to the other side, then quickly looked back over his shoulder. The grin had left his face, but there was no sign of fear. Sasan's mind and hands were busy keeping the tiny boat

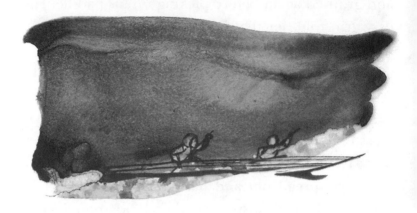

upright and on its course. But still she found time to smile and call out above the sound of the wind, "Keep your paddle moving and watch the wind. It won't take long to get through."

Sasan had been out during a storm once before. But that time she had been in the front hole. Then one of the older men had sat in back telling her what to do and what to watch for. Now everything was different. Now Sidak was counting on her to tell him what to do and what to watch for.

As their paddles drove them forward into the heart of the storm, the wind and waves beat down on the tiny boat. Water poured over it from every side. Only the raincoats, tied firmly over the holes, kept it from filling with water. Then to make things even worse, the clouds seemed to open up. Sheets of water driven by the howling wind slashed against Sasan's face. For a moment she could not see and all seemed lost. But she did not stop fighting the storm. During those seconds when she was almost blinded, she depended on the motion of her body in the boat. This told her where the paddle was needed to keep it from flipping all the way over.

When Sasan's eyes cleared, she caught a quick glimpse of Sidak. He, too, was using the motion of his body to guide his paddle. "Our ways will bring us safely through the storm," she said to herself with a new feeling of strength.

To Sasan the next minutes seemed like a lifetime. The wind did not let up for a moment. At times it changed direction so quickly it seemed to be coming from all sides at once. The waves, lashed by the changing wind, tossed them about like a bobbing cork. And the rain continued pounding against their faces, making it almost impossible to see. But through all this, the feeling of strength stayed with her. As the minutes passed, this feeling grew even stronger. She saw her brother's paddle move from side to side to where it was needed, and without any word from her. Together they made a team that would win out over wind and sea.

After a while the wind lessened and the worst of the storm was over. The rain still poured down, but it no longer blinded Sasan. Now she could easily pick out a path across the rough waters. She relaxed and her thoughts turned to long-ago times—those times when men took boats just like hers and traveled hundreds of miles over open water in search of fish and seals. She, like them, had won out over the terrible storms that had their birthplace among these islands of her people.

Sasan's thoughts were stopped short by Sidak's voice. Above the sound of the wind she heard him yell, "We made it. This boat is better than the new ones with their outboard motors." He, too, was proud of what they had done.

Sasan's feelings of pride and happiness were brought to a quick end. While Sidak's face was still turned toward her, the boat slid up onto the crest of a big wave. Just before it tipped downward, and while the bow was still out of the water, a sudden gust of wind from the left lifted the bow still higher. The whole boat rolled over on its side. Neither Sasan nor her brother was ready. Too late, Sidak swung around and jabbed the water with his paddle. It did no good. He was too high up out of the water to help roll it back over.

Now it was up to Sasan. Swiftly she pushed her paddle into the water and pulled back up with all her might. By this time her right arm was already under water. She could feel water press against her side as it tried to find its way through the raincoat. With her feet braced against a bottom rib of the boat and the paddle in just the right place, she held on with all her strength. In a moment the gust let up, the bow came down to where Sidak could use his paddle again, and together they rolled the boat over off its side.

They had won out over the storm a second time. But this time there was no talking. They paddled silently and without stopping until they were completely out of the storm's grasp. The sea was still rough, but the wind had lessened, the rain had stopped, and the clouds had lifted. Sasan now knew she had nothing more to fear. She felt even better when she looked toward shore and saw the steep, rocky cliffs of East Peak give way to green rolling hills. Sarana Bay was not far off.

When the boat at last slipped into the quiet waters of

the bay and its bow touched against the sandy shore, Sasan felt a great joy in her heart. A joy not just over what she and her brother had done, but for the Old Ways. For her people who had learned these ways and passed them on. And for Grandmother who had held to the Old Ways when others had laughed at her for doing so. In her great joy and thankfulness she called out, "Sidak, we won."

Sidak had already untied his raincoat from around the front hole and stood on the beach facing her. He said nothing, but his face told her everything she wanted to know.

Now that they had at last reached their summer camp, the dangers of the last hour or so were quickly forgotten. Sasan thought of all the things that needed to be done.

"Where will we start?" she asked. Then because she neither wanted or expected an answer, she went on, "Sidak, you must check the fish trap and put the stakes back. I will take the things up to our place and get the beds ready for tonight." She looked out over the bay, then added, "We must hurry. It will be dark soon and we brought no lantern."

Sasan carried the first load to their summer home but did not open the door and go in. Instead she put

everything down and stood looking at this house
which she and Grandmother always called by its old
name "barabara." It was so different from the new
house their father had built for them in the village.
This one was a low sod shed made from the grassy
earth which could be dug up almost anywhere on the
island. The barabara was a house built in the Old Way
except for the modern door and window. She
remembered Grandmother saying, "This house is
built from the earth of our island. These earth walls
keep out both the wind and the rain."

As Sasan opened the door and went in, she
thought of these things that Grandmother had said.
Once inside, the wonderful smell of dried grass met
her and brought back other memories. She remembered the years past when Grandmother would open
the door and they would step inside in this same way.
Everything would always be just as they had left it the
fall before. It was as if time had stood still. The home-
made table and benches stood there waiting to be
used. The pots and pans hung on the wall just where
she and Grandmother had left them. The tiny cookstove needed its pipes put back up, but the grass beds
at the back of the room were fluffed up and ready to
be slept in. And last of all, she looked at the clean

earth floor. Grandmother had always expected her to sweep the floor just before leaving. But this past fall, for the first time, Sasan had not done it. She could not remember why she had argued with Grandmother about having to do it. In the end Grandmother had done it herself. It was a painful memory now. Sasan was glad when Sidak stuck his head in the door and asked, "It's almost dark, why didn't you bring all the things in?"

Together they brought in what was left. Then, when Sidak mentioned he was hungry, Sasan put out on the table the smoked fish she had brought along. As they sat silently in the gathering darkness eating the fish, Sasan saw a look of sadness come over her brother's face. She asked, "Do you remember what Grandmother always used to say when we were unhappy or in pain?"

"Yes," Sidak answered, "she used to say, 'The wind is not a river.'"

Sasan said, "Yes, it is true. The sadness we feel today, like the wind in the storm we just passed through, must also pass away." As she said these words she tried hard not to show the pain and sadness in her own heart.

THE VISITORS

Sasan awoke early the next morning. It was still dark when she opened her eyes, but the light of early dawn was already creeping in the small window. The warm grass bed felt good, and she tried to go back to sleep. Her eyes closed but her mind was wide awake. Heavy breathing from across the room told her that Sidak was still sleeping. He always slept soundly and never got up without Grandmother first giving him a good scolding.

The thought of Grandmother made her eyes open

wide. Everything that had happened the day before ran through her mind. She crawled out of bed, straightened her dress, and put on her shoes. Then she went to the door, opened it, and stepped outside. A thick fog covered the bay. Sasan stood for a moment taking in the stillness that hung over the camp. A lone gull glided past and landed on the beach only a few feet from her. Without making a sound, it walked over to the mouth of the small creek that emptied into the bay. Sasan followed it until she came to the dam and the fish trap that her brother had gotten ready the night before. The gull jumped up on the fish trap but did not move when Sasan came near. She was glad the bird was there to share her loneliness. As she sat on a rock, a splash in the water behind the dam told her a fish had been trapped there during the night. She made no move to take it out and ready it for the drying rack. Her brother could do that later.

The sky grew lighter and soon she could see the low hill on the other side of the creek. For a moment she thought of walking to the top of the hill and exploring the old barabaras there. These had been lived in by her people a long time ago and were now covered with tall grass. But she did not go. Her troubled mind kept her sitting there in silence.

As time passed, a breeze sprang up and brought a spatter of rain from a low hanging cloud. At the same time, Sasan at last came to understand what was troubling her. Quickly she went back and woke up her brother. "Sidak," she said, "hurry and get up. We are going back to the village."

"But why?" he asked.

"I have been troubled all morning and now I know why," she answered.

"But why do you want to leave now? We just got here. There are things to be done. I must check to see if there are fish in the trap." He thought for a moment, then added, "I'm hungry. Let's eat and then talk about it."

A firmness came into Sasan's voice. "There is not time," she said. "The fish will stay alive until Monday. We will take the trail back and eat smoked fish on the way."

"But you still have not told me why we must go back now."

As Sasan got things together, she said, "Every Sunday since I can remember Grandmother has expected both of us to be in church. We will not disappoint her on this very first Sunday when she is no longer with us. If we leave now, we can still be there in time."

"But why not take the boat?"

"It would not be any faster," she answered. "And besides, it is too early in the morning to know whether there might be storms near the cliffs at East Peak today."

Sidak said no more and in a few minutes they were walking the trail along Lake Nicholas. He found it hard to keep up with his sister and grumbled, but it did little good. At last, after walking over an hour without stopping, they came to where the trail branched. The south fork led to the other side of the island, to Massacre Bay. It was seldom used. The north fork led to the village. Here, Sasan decided they would rest. Another hour and they would be back at the village, and still in time for church.

The fog had lifted, but a low cloud layer shut out the sun and covered the mountain peaks around them. A strong, steady wind blew from the south, but Sasan and Sidak found a comfortable spot in a small ditch. Here they kept out of the wind while they rested. Sidak was still hungry and ate some more of the smoked fish while Sasan closed her eyes and tried to rest. As she lay there, she kept thinking about

Grandmother who was now gone forever and about her father who was far away. Now she was expected to take care of herself and her brother.

"I don't want to," she said aloud.

Sidak looked up in surprise. Sasan opened her eyes and explained, "I was just talking to myself."

"I know," Sidak answered, "but what were you thinking about?"

She was quiet for a moment then said, "Our last letter from Father was sent from Cold Bay. Do you think he will be on the first boat and that he will stay?"

"He might if we both ask him to."

When his sister said nothing, he went on, "What if the boat came in last night and he's there right now waiting for us?"

"Sidak, you are being foolish," she answered back. "It is too early for the boat to come. Besides, the radio at the school said Japanese planes bombed Dutch Harbor only a few days ago. If the war is that close, maybe no boats will come."

Neither one said anything for a time. A wren's trill broke the silence, then everything was still again except for the wind rustling the dry stems of the dead grass.

After another silence, Sasan said, "Remember, from now on until Father comes, you are to do as I say. You promised Grandmother you would."

Sidak lowered his head and said nothing. A moment later Sasan's ears picked up a humming sound. At first it was mixed with the blowing of the wind through the grass, but soon it grew louder. As it did, Sidak sat up. "It's an airplane!" he said. "Remember? The Navy sent an airplane to our village last year." She heard the excitement in his voice as he went on, "Maybe a Navy plane is bringing Father home."

Sasan did not want her brother to build up his hopes, but she did not know what to say. Sidak was right—it was an airplane. Now it was circling above them and only the cloud layer kept them from seeing it. They both listened and the plane kept circling. After some time, the sound moved away and slowly faded.

"It didn't land," Sidak said slowly.

Sasan tried to cheer him up by saying, "No, it did not. Perhaps the fog in the harbor was still too thick. It will come back." Then she changed to something else, "We must leave now if we want to get back to the village in time for church."

In the moment of quiet that followed, Sasan heard another strange sound. Sidak did not hear it and started getting up out of the ditch. She put a hand on his arm and pulled him back down, motioning for him to be quiet. Soon the sound grew louder.

"What is it?" he whispered.

"I don't know. It sounds likes voices," Sasan whispered back. "It is coming from the Massacre Bay trail."

"But why would anyone from the village be down that way?" Sidak thought for a moment, then added, "Maybe some of the men left the village last night to hunt ducks."

Sasan shook her head. "You forget, there are no good lakes down that way."

They stopped whispering and listened again. Sasan

wanted to look up over the edge of the ditch, but she was afraid. She could hear men's voices but could not understand any of their words. She touched her brother's arm and whispered, "These are not our people, but they could be American soldiers. We must not let them see us until we find out who they are."

Both of them crawled into the dead grass and lay next to each other with their heads on the ground. The voices were quite loud now and there were many of them. Sasan's heart pounded as she listened. The ditch they were hiding in was close to where the trail forked, and some of the men were already quite near. She closed her eyes tightly and tried to understand their words. Two of them were talking, but they were not using English or Aleut. "Who can they be?" she asked herself. There were no other people on Attu and no one lived on the nearby islands. Navy men lived on the island of Kiska, but they spoke English.

Then Sasan thought again of the news on the school radio about the bombing of Dutch Harbor and the truth came to her at once. These were Japanese soldiers. They were coming to capture her village. They were coming to take over this island which had been the home of her people for so many years. She opened her eyes and looked into her brother's face lying next to hers. She saw that he, too, knew.

Sasan's worry about the village and the island had made her forget for a moment the danger of being seen. The thought of this danger returned suddenly when the men on the trail stopped right next to where they were hiding. Two of them seemed to be arguing. They were standing where the trail forked. If some of the soldiers took the trail toward Sarana Bay, they could easily see into the ditch. The dead grass would not be thick enough to hide Sasan and Sidak.

Sasan pressed her body down hard against the ground and her heart began beating even faster. The two men went on arguing and were joined by a third. There were men all along the trail now. They seemed to be waiting. Many were talking in low voices, and from time to time one of them laughed.

At last the men who were arguing stopped their loud talk. Sasan felt better. Now, she thought, they will move on. If some of them take the trail to Sarana Bay, they will either see us or they won't. We can do nothing more.

But the men did not move on. They seemed to be taking a short rest. Sasan heard some of them walking through the dead grass on the side of the trail. She inched her hand toward her brother's arm without moving her head. When she felt his arm, she pressed it and lay still again. Suddenly, from almost right above her, she heard a man's voice. She held her breath and her fingers dug deeply into Sidak's jacket. The voice stopped, but without looking, Sasan knew the man was standing with his feet right above her head. Then just as suddenly, it was all over. Someone shouted and the man moved quickly away. All talking stopped and Sasan heard the slapping of hands against wood or something hard. "They must be picking up their rifles," she thought. Another shout and the men began moving.

Sasan wanted so much to turn her head so she could see whether any of them were taking the trail to Sarana Bay. But she dared not. And so she waited for something to happen, still holding tightly to her brother's arm.

Minutes passed and there was still no end to the line of soldiers. During every passing second Sasan waited for the shout that would tell her that some soldier's eyes had found their hiding place. No one shouted and after a while she began to relax. Slowly she turned her head and looked over toward the

Sarana Bay trail. It was empty. They were safe.

Not too much later Sasan heard the last soldiers pass and their voices disappear up the main trail toward the village. Slowly she lifted her head off the ground, sat up, then raised her head inch by inch above the ditch. First she looked to the left. The trail toward Massacre Bay was empty. Then she looked to the right. A long line of soldiers in brown uniforms was moving up the trail to Attu Village. All of them carried rifles. The very last men were carrying machine guns.

Sasan whispered down to her brother, "They have gone. You can look now."

Sidak sat up quickly and looked toward the village. He sat there staring after the soldiers, saying nothing. Sasan saw bits of grass clinging to the side of his face and tried to brush them off. He pushed her hand away and kept staring. At last he turned towards his sister and asked, "What will happen now?"

Sasan had already asked herself the same question, and the answer filled her with dread.

THE VILLAGE IS TAKEN

For a moment Sasan did not move. Everything was again just as it had been a short time ago. Just as it had been when they first crawled into the ditch to rest. Everything was quiet except for the sound of the south wind blowing through the grass. The low clouds still covered the mountain peaks, just as before. But in that short time, Sasan's world had been turned upside down. News of the bombing, just a few days ago, had made her feel sad for the men who had died. But the war and the bombing had seemed so far

away; not a part of her world. Her island was far out
in the ocean. The thick fogs, heavy rains, and strong
winds kept all ships away except for the one or two
that brought supplies each year. Yet now, on this
Sunday morning, enemy soldiers had landed. In
another hour they would capture the village. Then
the island would no longer belong to her people.

Sasan did not think long about these things. In a
moment she stood up and spoke, "Our island is in
danger. We must do something."

"What can we do?" asked Sidak. "Even if we could
warn the men in the village, they have no guns. They
could not fight against so many."

Sasan answered, "We cannot warn them. It is too
late and there is only one trail. We will have to follow
them and see what happens. Then we can decide
what to do next."

Just as they were ready to start, the loud call of a
raven came from somewhere ahead. At the same
moment a sudden cold gust of wind swept off the
snow-covered mountain peaks, whipped against
Sasan's dress, and sent a shiver through her body.

"We can start now," she said, and they began walking.

No bushes grew along the trail, and the new grass
was not yet tall enough to help hide them. Sasan

stopped from time to time to make sure they did not follow too closely after the marching soldiers.

When they reached the hill overlooking the village and the harbor, they stopped and crawled behind a large rock to watch. Sasan had come to this same place many times before to be by herself. From here she could see the houses standing along the shore of the harbor, sheltered from the strong winds by East Peak on one side and West Peak on the other.

Now as she watched, everything was still quiet and peaceful. But it would not be so for long. Already the soldiers had formed a line in back of the village. The line ran from the church at one end, nearest East Peak, to the school at the other end. It was already too late for anyone to escape into the mountains. Another line of soldiers was moving along the beach in front of the village. When the two lines met, there would be a circle of soldiers all around it. Everyone would be trapped inside this circle.

Sasan and Sidak watched and listened for a sign that someone in the village had at last seen the danger, but nothing happened. The soldiers seemed to move without making a sound. "Why doesn't someone see them?" she asked herself. Sasan's heart pounded as she watched and waited. "Are all the people still in church?" she wondered.

They did not have much longer to wait and wonder. A shot rang out in the morning air, then another. Sasan felt her brother's hand against her arm, but her eyes did not leave the village. People started pouring out of the houses and out of the grass-covered barabaras next to the church. Some of the older people still used these as homes. They all ran together into groups and stood staring at the soldiers. The soldiers walked with their rifles pointed straight ahead, making the circle smaller and smaller.

Sasan had almost forgotten that Sidak was with her. When he whispered, "Do you suppose any of the men got away?" it surprised her and she jumped.

Before she could answer, another shot rang out. It seemed to come from the school which sat off by itself, next to the stream that emptied into the harbor. Two soldiers ran inside the school, their rifles ready. One more shot came from inside, then all was quiet again.

Sasan's eyes turned back to the people in the village. By this time the soldiers had pushed them together into one tight circle. The women, some holding babies, stood in the middle along with the younger children. Around the outside the men stood facing the soldiers. The soldiers held their rifles pointed at the men. The end of each rifle held a knife blade and these were almost touching the circle of men.

Sasan could hear nothing, and for a moment nothing seemed to be happening. No one moved. Then suddenly, a soldier raised his rifle in the air and brought it down against one of the men. The man fell backward into the crowd and two other village men grabbed at the soldier and his rifle. Sasan heard a shot, then saw other soldiers rush in and push the two village men back inside the circle.

Sidak's fingers tightened on Sasan's arm again as he said, "I have seen enough. I will go down and stand together with the men of the village."

Sasan felt her own anger grow as she watched the enemy soldiers. But she answered, "You must not go. As you see, the men can do nothing against so many. And what can they fight with? There is only one gun and that is in the school."

When he did not answer, Sasan looked and saw the anger on his face. The hand still holding her arm trembled as he said, "Would you want me to just sit here and watch them kill our people?"

She answered, "Remember, we may be the only ones who are still free. We must plan well what we do."

Sidak said no more and their eyes turned back to the village. Chief Joseph now stood facing one of the soldiers. This one was dressed differently and had a sword hanging from his side. The two of them talked. After a short time, Chief Joseph turned toward his people. Then the soldiers moved back and the people walked slowly to their homes.

After all the families were back inside, the soldiers began to gather around the one who was dressed differently. He seemed to be their leader. Just then, out of the corner of her eye, Sasan saw one of the village men run from his house and dash towards the barabaras over by the church. He was almost there before one of the soldiers saw him. He quickly aimed his rifle and there was the sound of a single shot as the man disappeared into the heavy grass between the houses. Sasan could not see if he had been hit. Soldiers swarmed over to the spot. Others moved in close to the other houses to make sure no one else tried to escape. A moment later the man came out with his hands over his head. Two soldiers pushed him forward with the blades of their rifles. They marched him toward the school where their leader was waiting.

After the man and the soldiers disappeared into the school, Sasan said, "You see, it does no good against so many."

Sidak's next words put a new fear into Sasan's heart. "We will see. Tonight in the darkness I will use my knife against the enemy."

Sasan answered quietly, "You are too young. And even if you did kill one of them, what good would that do?"

"I will not just sit here and wait," he answered back, "I will do something."

A firmness that her brother had never before heard came into Sasan's voice. "You are angry," she said. "But you will obey me as you promised Grandmother you would. You must do nothing without telling me first." Then she said more gently, "Together we will think of a way to free our people."

Sidak spoke no more, but his face was still filled with anger.

Hours passed as the two lay by the rock on the hilltop, watching and saying nothing. The sky stayed cloudy and by midafternoon the wind had shifted to the north, bringing with it a lower layer of clouds and heavy rain showers from off the sea. The north wind also brought the sound of heavy waves crashing against the rocks at the harbor's mouth. From time to time Sasan would look over and see the waves throw themselves against the rocks, sending water and spray in all directions. But most of the time her eyes were on the village.

The people were all still in their homes. A machine gun now stood at each end of the village; one next to the church, the other near the school. And there were soldiers everywhere. Two sat by each gun and watched. Some were marching at both the front and the back of the village to make sure no one came outside. Others were busy chopping away the dead beach grass in back of the houses so that anyone trying to run away into the mountains could be seen by the guards. Still others were rolling wire out from the school and putting up a searchlight next to one of the machine guns.

Sasan saw all this: the many soldiers, the machine guns, the searchlight, and her people waiting helplessly inside their houses. She saw all this and said, "It will be hard to free our people even after it is dark."

Sidak answered angrily, "Grandmother was wrong!"

"Why do you say that?" she asked.

Without looking at her he said, "Grandmother made us learn the Old Ways, but what good are they to us now? Will knowing how to use the bidarki help us fight the enemy? Will these ways help us free our people?"

Sasan answered quietly, "Do not mock. These ways can help us even now."

Sidak gave a short laugh. "They can help us? How?"

"Our ways have taught us how to find food and to live off the land. We will use what we have learned. We will stay hidden from the enemy soldiers as our people hid from their enemies long ago."

Before Sasan could go on Sidak asked, "And what good will it do for us to be free on our island? To be free while our people are held against their will in their own houses?"

Sasan looked over at her brother. His eyes were still on the village. She went on, "How many times has Grandmother told us the story of our men who lived long ago? What they did when the Russians forced them to hunt? They did not try to kill. They had only spears and the Russians had guns. No, they waited until the Russians were not watching, then they took their families and ran off into the hills. The people on the islands to the east did not learn to wait and many of them were killed."

When Sasan had finished, Sidak took his eyes off the village. He looked at her and said, "Tonight after dark, I will go down into the village and free the men. Then they can take their families and go into the mountains where the soldiers cannot find them."

Sasan thought for a time about what her brother had said, then answered, "It is one of the things we might do to help. But we cannot do it tonight."

"Why not tonight?" he asked.

"You have seen the soldiers, the machine guns, and the light. It will not be easy to get into the village and free our people. We must have a plan."

There was now anger in her brother's voice as he said, "I have a plan. I will go first to the barabaras. There the soldiers cannot see me as well. I will go to

Chief Joseph. His two oldest sons can help me free the other men."

Sasan listened but would not agree. "Surely the soldiers will put locks on the doors. How will you open them? And what of the machine gun and the light which are right next to the houses?" She stopped but not long enough for her brother to answer. "No, we will wait and think more about these things. If we do go, we must not fail."

Sidak's eyes were once more on the village. "I will not wait too long," he said.

These last words angered Sasan. She stood up behind the rock and said, "We have other things to do now. It is late. The rain clouds are already moving in from the sea, and we have no food and no shelter for the night."

Sidak stood up too but did not look at her. She went on, "We will go back to camp first and make ready to live off the land."

Little more was said as they walked back over the trail to Sarana Bay. It was late and a light rain was falling when they finally heard the sounds of the sea. As they came to the last bend in the trail, Sasan, who was walking in front, stopped, turned around, and whispered, "It is best we leave the trail here and make sure there are no soldiers in the camp."

Crawling through the grass they soon came to a low mound. Here they could look and listen without being seen. Sasan peered out over the top and saw low clouds and fog rolling in over the waters of the bay. Wind rattled the dry grass on top of the mound and a sudden gust splattered rain against her face. All at once she felt terribly tired and hungry. Her wet clothes chilled her body, and she hoped with all her might the enemy soldiers had not found the summer camp.

Their boat was still there, high up on the beach where she and Sidak had left it the night before. There were no other boats to be seen. Everything seemed to be just as they had left it this morning. Still she was not sure. Motioning her brother to stay, she started walking to their house, carefully looking around as she went. When she opened the door and stepped inside, there was just enough light to tell her nothing had been moved. Next she went outside and walked along the sandy beach. There were no tracks since the last tide.

When she was sure of everything, she called to Sidak. As he walked towards her, she saw that he, too, was wet, tired, and hungry. Her earlier anger was forgotten. She smiled and said, "We will have a warm, dry place tonight."

Sidak, too, had forgotten his anger. He smiled back but said nothing.

"I know you are hungry," Sasan said, "but we must save the food we brought with us last night. Come, it is still light enough to look for sea urchins along the beach."

They found many of these round shellfish on the rocky beach above the creek. As they found some, they ate. The spiny shells cracked easily on the rocks, and they swallowed the yellow insides right from the shell. Sasan did not mind the taste. Grandmother had made her eat them since she was a baby.

LIVING OFF THE LAND

Sasan woke up with a start and looked over to see light coming through the window. She scrambled out of bed and called to her brother, "Hurry, wake up! We slept too late."

Sidak sat up grumbling and rubbing his eyes. Sasan was already at work, sorting the things they had brought from the village. Some of these she put into the two packsacks lying on the floor; the rest she placed to one side.

Again she called out, "Hurry, Sidak, straighten out the grass on the beds and take the stovepipe back down."

"But why?" he asked.

Sasan kept on packing things as she answered, "We are leaving here and setting up camp behind East Peak. From there we can watch the village and make plans."

Sidak was glad to be going back to the village and began hurrying, too, but he asked, "Why must we be in such a hurry?"

"Because yesterday the enemy soldiers saw the trail leading to this place. Soon they will send someone to see if there are people living here. We must go quickly and leave no signs that we were here."

Together they soon finished what needed to be done. They hid the boat in the tall grass, then put the things to be left behind under the boat. At last they were ready to leave. Sasan, wearing her raincoat and with her pack on her back, took one last look around. She wanted to make sure they had left no sign. Satisfied, she turned to Sidak. "Even now there might be soldiers on the trail," she said. "If there are, we must see them first. So watch and listen, and do not talk."

Sidak nodded and they started off. They had gone only a few steps when he said, "We haven't eaten yet."

Sasan turned to face her brother. "We must save

the food we brought from the village and learn to live off the land."

Sidak asked, "Is there time to eat some sea urchins? There are many, and it won't take long."

Sasan looked around and listened, then answered, "I do not hear anyone on the trail. We can hurry and gather some then take them with us and eat when we stop to rest."

Leaving their packs, they went to the rocky beach across the creek and quickly set to work. When they had gathered enough, Sasan tied them up in her scarf. Soon they were on their way again.

It had rained all night and everything was wet and dripping. A heavy fog kept Sasan from seeing far ahead on the trail. She was glad there was no wind. If they walked quietly, they could hear anyone who might be coming towards them.

The packs were heavy and Sidak was hungry, so they stopped halfway to the fork. There they rested and ate. Breaking the shells with a rock made a loud sound in the still morning air, and Sasan was glad when they had finished.

They were almost past Lake Nicholas when Sasan stopped and listened. She clearly heard voices far ahead on the trail. Quickly she motioned for her brother to follow her. They found a good hiding place behind some rocks and bushes along the shore of the lake. Here they slid off their packs and waited.

As the voices slowly grew louder, Sasan placed herself behind a thick bush where she could see the trail without being seen. She did not have long to wait. Walking towards her out of the fog, one behind the other, came three enemy soldiers. All three carried rifles over their shoulders, but none acted as though they planned to use them. The two in back were talking and laughing as they walked.

Sasan was surprised to see that two of them were very young. Except for their uniforms, they looked very much like the young men of her own village. They were sturdy and had dark skins and black hair. The older man walking in front seemed to be in charge. As they passed by, he turned his head and said something to the other two. This stopped their talking and laughing. But they were very close now, and Sasan saw the one in the middle turn and smile at the other. This told her they were still in a playful mood and did not fear the older man. As they walked away down the trail, the two young ones began talking again and the older one did not seem to mind.

When their voices could no longer be heard, Sasan

spoke, "I cannot believe they are enemy soldiers. They look and act so much like our own young men. And the older man, didn't he sound just like Father when he scolds us?"

Sasan had been still watching the trail as she spoke and was surprised when her brother answered with anger in his voice, "You think they are no different from our own men? Have you forgotten yesterday? Have you forgotten what they have done?" He did not give her time to answer. As he picked up his pack, he went on, "They are the enemy!"

Sasan saw that he was angry over what she had said and spoke no more. She picked up her pack and started walking.

It was almost noon when they left the trail near the village and started toward East Peak. The fog was gone and the clouds had lifted so that only the tops of the mountains were hidden. They moved slowly and kept behind rocks as much as possible to keep from being seen by anyone in the village. Soon they came to a place on the side of East Peak where they were well hidden, but close enough to watch the enemy soldiers below.

Sasan was glad to take off her pack and rest. She lay back for a moment and closed her eyes. When she opened them a few minutes later, her brother was already lying on his stomach next to a rock, watching.

"What are they doing?" she asked.

Sidak did not answer so she crawled over next to him and began watching too. Little had changed since the day before. Her people were still in their homes, the machine guns stood at each end of the village, and soldiers walked back and forth in front and in back of the houses. The barabaras were built into the side of the hills, and there the soldiers guarded only the fronts.

Thinking now of her brother's plan to enter the village and free the men, Sasan said, "On a night when the fog is thick, we could go down the hill in back of the church and get between the barabaras without being seen. Also, there is a hole under the church where we can hide. I have used it many times when we played hide-and-seek."

Sidak nodded his head and kept watching.

"But how will we free the people?" Sasan asked. "The soldiers may have put locks on the doors."

Sidak spoke at last, "We do not know that."

"But what if they have, what will we do then?"

Sidak did not answer, so Sasan talked of something else, "There do not seem to be as many soldiers today.

I have counted only twelve."

Sidak said, "The three that we met on the trail will be back. Also, I saw some standing at the window in the schoolhouse."

Just then a number of soldiers came out of the school. All of them carried rifles. As Sasan and Sidak watched, each one went over to one of the soldiers guarding the houses and took his place. Those who were through keeping watch then went back to the school.

"Now we know there are almost thirty," Sasan said.

Sidak answered with his eyes still on the village, "It does not matter how many. Chief Joseph's sons are strong and have learned the Old Ways well. If I free them, they will take the enemy by surprise and kill them one by one."

Again Sasan heard the deep anger in her brother's voice. She answered, "It would be better if we could free our people without killing."

Sidak became even more angry when he heard this. "Yes, it would be better if our people did not have to kill. But it would be even better if the enemy did not come to kill us. Have you forgotten yesterday? How the soldier shot at one of the men when he tried to run away?"

Sasan did not know how to answer. At last she said, "If the doors are not locked, then some night, when a heavy fog comes in off the water, our own men will escape and kill the enemy. The light will do little good on such a night."

A raven floated by close over their heads as Sasan waited for Sidak to speak. When he said nothing, she went on, "If the doors are locked, then on such a night we will go down into the village and free our people. So you see, we must first find out about the doors."

"How can we find that out without going down into the village?"

Sasan answered, "They must let our people out of their homes sometime during the day. We will watch from here. When they do open the doors, we will see how it is done."

Sidak said, "But we must know by tonight."

Sasan was just ready to tell her brother that he must obey her when the soldier with the sword came out of the school. He walked across the village and stopped in front of Chief Joseph's barabara. He knocked, then slid something back away from the doorknob and waited. Chief Joseph came out and stood for a moment talking, then went back inside.

Sasan and Sidak watched carefully as the bolt was put back in place.

Sidak turned to Sasan with a satisfied smile on his face. "The doors are bolted from the outside but not locked. It will be easy to slide back the bolt and open the doors tonight."

"You have forgotten about the light," Sasan answered. "We will go down tonight only if there is a fog."

A stubbornness came across Sidak's face. "And what if there is no fog for many nights?" he asked.

"Then we will wait," Sasan answered. "You must remember, we are probably the only ones free. What we do, we must do well." She paused for a moment, then added, "If we must, we will take the boat all the way to Kiska. The Navy men there have a radio. They will get someone to help us free our people."

Sidak was now looking at her. "I will not wait too long," he said.

Sasan's firmness turned to anger. "You will obey me because Grandmother told you to," she said. Then her anger softened and she added, "We will not have to wait long. It is spring and during this time there are few nights when the fog does not come in from the sea and cover our village."

With these words, she moved back behind the rock and started putting on her pack. "Come," she said, "we have seen enough. It is time to find a good place to camp on the other side of the peak, away from the village."

Sidak said nothing, but anger still showed on his face. He picked up his pack and made ready to go. Sasan stood behind the rock and took one more look down toward the village. As she did, her eye caught something dark on the trail that came up from Sarana Bay. "Look," she said, "the soldiers are returning from our camp. I hope they did not find our boat."

Sidak looked to where she pointed, but still did not speak.

The next half hour was spent crawling between rocks and keeping out of sight of the village as they worked their way around the peak. When they finally reached the other side and could not be seen, Sasan stood up and looked around.

She knew and loved every part of these mountains that circled the village and the harbor. After their mother had died, Grandmother had taken her and her brother up into these places many times. In early spring she had taken them to find duck and sea gull eggs. In summer she had taken them to the hillsides for the special grass she used for weaving her beautiful baskets. And in fall she had taken them into those same hills for the many berries and plants which they used for food. After a moment, Sasan pushed these thoughts aside and started walking.

It was early afternoon, the sun was trying to break through the clouds, and a slight wind was blowing when they came to the spot Sasan was looking for. Rocks rose up on three sides and sheltered it from the winds driving up the cliffs of the sea. Two of the rocks formed a low, cave-like opening which would keep the rain out in even the stormiest weather.

Sasan took off her pack and sat down. Sidak took off his, then walked over to where he could look down on the cliffs. His back was to her, but she could tell from the way he stood that he was still angry. She wanted so much to have someone to talk to, but she knew her brother was not the one. His only thought was to go down to the village tonight to free the men. She did not know what to do with him. He was so young and stubborn and he did not understand. If only the fog would come in from the sea tonight.

The two of them said nothing for some time. Then, at last, Sasan thought of a way to keep her brother busy for the rest of the day while she decided on a plan. "Sidak," she asked, "could you find your way to Sarana Bay from here without using the trail?"

Sidak turned around and showed interest at once. "Alexi and I went that way last summer. Except for a few places, it is easy and much shorter." He paused a moment, then asked, "Why?"

"I would like to know if the boat is still safe. If the soldiers found it and the extra things we hid under it, they might wonder. If they do think there is someone free on the island, they will surely guard the village more carefully." A faint smile came to her face as she went on, "Also, there are fish in the trap. If you clean one and bring it back, I will have a small fire ready. I think both of us would like cooked fish better than more raw sea urchins."

It did not take Sidak long to empty his pack and be on his way. Sasan called after him, "Do not forget to leave everything as you found it in case the soldiers come back."

Setting up camp only took a few minutes. All that needed to be done was to arrange a good fireplace, find some crowberry bushes, which would make a fire without smoke, and lay out some dead grass to dry in the wind so they would have a comfortable bed tonight. She had finished two of the tasks and was walking down toward the cliffs looking for crowberry bushes when she heard a low humming sound. She thought almost at once of the airplane that flew over yesterday. Today, however, it was different. Yesterday she wanted to see the plane, because she thought it would be the Navy. Today she didn't want to see it, because it might be the enemy. Today, too, the clouds were high and the plane would be flying under them and close to the ground.

Quickly she looked around for a place to hide. Her camp with all its large rocks was too far away. Around her lay the sloping, flat hillside covered with dead grass, but all of it too short to hide under. The sound was plainly coming from the other side of the peak, the village side, and was getting louder and louder.

Sasan stood there looking from side to side, looking for something that wasn't there. When the sound was almost upon her, she at last caught sight of a small black rock almost completely covered with dead grass. She rushed to it, pulled the grass away and pressed herself against one of its higher sides. She lay there out of breath, her heart pounding. A moment later the sound of the plane's engine thundered down upon her. Then the plane itself flew low over where she was lying. She caught a glimpse of the red rising suns painted on each wing tip. It was an enemy plane. She turned her head slowly, watching to see if it would circle and come back. It did not, and soon disappeared over the ridge toward Sarana Bay.

Sasan went on down the hillside, found a crowberry bush and tore off some branches, then hurried back to her camp. The rest of the afternoon was spent worrying about whether her brother had hidden before the plane reached him.

Sidak returned late. He was tired but in good spirits. "Is the boat safe?" she asked.

"They did not go anywhere near it," he answered.

Sasan then asked, "The plane, did you hear it in time?"

Sidak answered, "It was easy. I did not let the enemy see me."

Sidak took a large salmon out of his pack. He removed the dry grass from around it and handed it to Sasan with a smile. Then he carefully started a small fire while Sasan cut the salmon into strips and laid them on a flat stone to cook. As they worked, Sasan asked more questions about his trip. She was pleased to see that his anger had left him.

It took some time before the fish strips were ready. Part of that time Sidak walked around outside the shelter keeping watch. He looked out to sea often and seemed restless. At last he came next to the fire and began putting things back in his pack. Sasan saw all this but said nothing.

Dusk was falling when the salmon was at last ready and they sat down to enjoy it. Little was said while they ate. When they were finished, Sasan kept the coals going and put more strips on so they would have cooked fish the next day.

At last Sidak said, "It is almost dark. While you cook the rest of the fish, I will go to the village side of the peak to see if the fog is moving in."

Sasan answered, "Sidak, you have been watching the wind and the skies. The wind has been blowing from the land for some time. You know no fog can come in from the sea with the wind from the south."

Sidak tried to hide his anger as he said, "The winds on our island change quickly and we must be ready."

"That is true," Sasan answered, "but your wishing will not make it happen." Then her voice softened. "Perhaps we can learn something by watching the village at night," she said. "Go, and I will come too after the fish strips are cooked."

A light wind was still blowing from the south when Sasan at last walked toward the place where Sidak sat watching. A full moon hung low over the sea and filled the night with a soft light. She sat down next to her brother and together they looked silently down at the village.

Below them the searchlight swept back and forth, lighting up the houses, the church, and the beach for just a moment as it passed. No light shone from any of the windows except at the schoolhouse.

Sasan's eyes moved from the village, across the harbor, to the sea. The moon's light showed no storm clouds hanging out over the water, waiting to move in and cover the island. Sasan knew it would do no good to wait, but she could not bring herself to tell Sidak. And so they sat watching.

Sasan was surprised when at last her brother said, "There is no reason for us to stay. We have seen where the soldiers walk and how often the light moves across the village." He paused, then said, "There will be no fog tonight."

When they stood up to go, Sasan said, "Before tomorrow night the wind will change and bring in rain and clouds from the sea. We will be ready. We will go first to my hiding place under the church. From there it is not far to Chief Joseph's barabara." Little more was said as they walked back to camp.

Later, Sasan crawled into the grass she had dried that afternoon and then looked over at Sidak. He was already sleeping. At last this long day was finally over. She closed her eyes and fell fast asleep.

THE NIGHT VISIT

Sasan opened her eyes wide. It felt as though someone had just awakened her and was still standing there. But it was dark, and she could see nothing. Then a feeling of dread came over her. Slowly she rolled over and reached out her hand toward her brother's bed. It was empty.

Her hands flew over the grass, throwing it in all directions. Sidak was nowhere in the shelter. She lay still a moment, her hand on the overturned grass. It still felt warm. "Perhaps he has just gotten up to go outside," she thought. She crawled out and looked around in the darkness. It was still a clear night, and beyond the shadows of the rock shelter she could see stars sparkling in the night sky.

Sasan called out, "Sidak?" There was no answer. She called again, "Sidak!" this time much louder. Moments more of waiting, and then the truth came to her. Her brother had gone down to the village.

Knowing the truth took away some of Sasan's dread and moved her into action. Taking only a moment to put on her shoes and jacket, she moved out of the shelter and headed toward the village. As she walked, she made her plans. It was a bad night to do what needed to be done. There was no fog to hide her, and no wind to drown out the sounds she made. But she must go down into the village after her brother. "If only it is not too late," she thought.

When she arrived at the other side of the peak, her eyes were drawn to the searchlight. Its finger of light was still sweeping from the hillside across the houses to the beach and then back again.

Sasan stood watching, just long enough to notice the darkness that always followed along after the moving light. She knew she would have to use well those brief moments of darkness.

When she came to the hillside right above the church, she slid down and reached the graveyard easily. Then she lay there a moment looking. The searchlight did not shine all the way around in back of the church. From there to the graveyard it was still quite dark. But from where she lay she could see the searchlight's beam sweep over to the barabaras, stop, then move back again. Just for a moment, she also saw a soldier with his rifle hung over his shoulder, looking towards the old grass-covered houses. Seeing how quickly the light returned and how the soldier stood with his eyes always on the doors of these houses, she knew that her brother should not have gone to Chief Joseph's first.

Sasan left her hiding place and moved farther down. Quickly she found the hole under the church. Moving the dead grass carefully from in front of it, she slid through. There was just enough room for her to crawl forward on her stomach across to the other side. There she was well hidden from the soldier and she could also see the front of Chief Joseph's barabara. It was the second one from the church. The soldier was still standing just a little past it. He kept turning his head from side to side, watching. With the light gone for just a few seconds, there was no way the bolt could be removed from any of the doors without the soldier knowing it. Yet Sasan knew that her brother was lying somewhere in the darkness, waiting to try it. "I will have to get to him before he does something foolish," she thought.

Quickly she crawled back across the hole, slid through, and moved along the wall till she came to the back corner of the church. As soon as the light disappeared, she dashed across the open space between the church and the first barabara. Just as she pressed herself against its grassy side, the light swept over her and away again. She caught her breath as she waited for its next sweep. Then she crawled up one of the grassy sides and down the other. By the time the light returned, she was already lying down and out of sight. Then she raised her head above the grass, ready to look for her brother when the light swept over again. This time Sasan saw him across from her and near Chief Joseph's door.

Sasan began slowly crawling through the grass toward him. She had just started when one of the flashes of light showed him facing her with a knife in his hand. She waited for the next flash of light to be sure he saw who it was. He did, and moved towards her. When he lay next to her at last, she whispered in

his ear, "It is too dangerous here. We must try somewhere else."

Before Sasan could say more, she heard voices, and
they both froze. The still night air made the voices
sound loud and close. Two soldiers were talking, but
there was no excitement and no shouting. Sasan
could tell they had not been seen, and some of the
fear left her. After a while she heard one of the soldiers walking away, then all was quiet again.

Through all this Sasan had kept her whole body
pressed against the ground. Now she raised her head
and looked around. She wanted to be sure no soldier
could see them when they began moving away. She
saw none and leaned over to whisper in Sidak's ear,
"Follow me to the hole under the church. There we
can hide and talk. I will go first, right after the light
leaves. You follow when it leaves the next time."

Sasan stood up, pressed herself against the grassy
wall of the house, and waited. The light flashed over,
then away, and she began climbing. Safely over, she
pressed against the other wall. The light came again
and in the darkness that followed she moved away
from the wall, ready to help her brother as he came
up over the top and down.

Now that her brother was safe again, Sasan's

thoughts were already on how to talk him out of trying to free any of the other men. But these thoughts
were ended by a loud snap in the darkness. A
moment later, before Sasan could imagine what had
happened, her brother slid down off the roof, land-
ing on his feet next to her.

Then she heard the soldier's loud shout. It came
from the other side of the grass-covered house.
Without a word, she grabbed her brother's hand and
started running across the open space toward the
church. As they ran, the light returned and fell full
upon them. But even worse to Sasan was the sound of
their running feet as it filled the still night air.

Their only safety lay in the friendly darkness in
back of the church. The light had passed by the time
they reached it. For just a moment Sasan thought of
running up the hill to the graveyard. Other shouts
and the sound of running feet ended this thought.
She pulled her brother toward the hole then crawled
through first and he right after her. Quickly she
squeezed herself and her brother in behind a mound
of dirt. Here they could not be seen if someone
should find the hole and flash a light inside.

Sasan's heart pounded and she gasped for air as
she lay waiting. Shouts seemed to be coming from all

sides at once. Then she heard voices nearby. They came from in front of the church, moved around to the back, then to the other side. They stopped by the hole and soon Sasan saw the beam of a flashlight move back and forth underneath the church. She held her breath. Everything was still for a moment. She kept her eyes open, but her head was pressed down against the mound, and she saw nothing but the light. The soldier was only a few feet from her, and the sound of his heavy breathing reached her ears. Then, just when she thought her lungs would burst, he spoke. At the same time the light went out, and she again heard talking, but now it was no longer close. A moment later the searchers moved along toward the front of the church and were gone.

The shouting soon died down, but the talking and the sound of soldiers walking around kept on. Sasan knew they were still looking. But she was no longer worried. They had already searched her hiding place. A short while later she heard voices up on the hillside in back of the church. "I am glad we did not run to the graveyard to hide," she said to herself.

At last the search seemed to slow down, and Sasan felt safe enough to move out of the uncomfortable place they had squeezed themselves into. She tugged at her brother's arm, and together they crawled over to the spot where she had watched from before. Here there was more room, and she could at last look out to see what was happening.

Everything seemed the same, except now the searchlight showed two soldiers. One was standing as before, facing the barabaras. The other one was walking. She watched as he walked along in front of the grass-covered houses then up the hillside in back, finally disappearing from sight in back of the church. A few minutes later he came out from in front of the church and started walking around the same circle all over again.

Sidak whispered, "They have stopped searching." Then, as if he already knew what she was about to ask, he said, "My knee broke a dry stick as I crawled over the top of the house."

Now that the greatest danger had passed and he was safely beside her once more, Sasan felt a strange joy mixed with anger towards her brother. She whispered back, "The noise could not be helped, but all this would not have happened if you had obeyed."

"Yes, it is true," he said, "next time I will do as I promised Grandmother I would."

The sorrow in her brother's voice and the harshness of her own words shamed Sasan. She squeezed his hand and whispered, "Grandmother would have scolded you as I just did. But she would also have admired you for your great courage."

Their whispering was cut short when Sasan again heard footsteps. She pressed her brother's arm, and they both listened. The steps passed by the front of the church. Then Sasan saw the soldier with the sword walk toward Chief Joseph's house. He did not speak to the one who was guarding, but knocked loudly, then raised the bolt from across the door and waited. After a while Chief Joseph himself opened the door and stepped out.

Sasan was surprised to hear the soldier ask in English, "You heard my men searching here among your houses?"

Chief Joseph nodded his head but did not speak.

The soldier went on, "The guard heard a noise, and when he called out, someone ran away into the darkness. We think there is someone on this island spying on us."

Chief Joseph shrugged his shoulders, and Sasan heard him say, "On still nights such as this, foxes often come down from the hills into our village. What your soldier heard was a pack of foxes. They ran because he scared them with his shouting."

The soldier thought for a moment, then said, "What you say may be true. But tomorrow morning early we will bring all your people together. Then I will want you to tell them what I have now told you. You must also tell them that when this person is caught, he will be treated as a spy. He will be put to death." He went on, "And you will also tell them that if any of your men try to escape and join this spy, they, too, will be put to death."

No more was said, and Chief Joseph went back inside. The soldier put the bolt back in place and walked away toward the school.

Sasan's thoughts quickly turned to the problem of getting back up the hillside. She whispered to her brother, "We can crawl over to the opening and wait.

When the soldier passes by, I will go out first and you follow. We will go as far as the graveyard while he is walking in front of the church. We will hide there while he is back on the hillside. When he is once more on the other side of the church, we can leave safely."

Sasan began to tremble as she lay next to the opening and heard the footsteps of the soldier coming toward her. He walked slowly, and it seemed as though her heart pounded harder with each step he took. At last he was right next to where she lay. She held her breath. In a moment she heard him moving away from her. Quickly she pushed her head out and watched until she saw the soldier's dark form disappear around the corner of the church. Then she was out of the hole and crawling through the darkness towards the graveyard. Sidak was right behind her.

When they reached the graveyard, Sasan stopped and looked back down. From where she lay she could see the searchlight sweeping back and forth. In its light she saw that the two soldiers were now talking. She tugged her brother's arm and together they continued going.

Far up the hillside, Sasan stopped and looked back. The searchlight still swept back and forth as before, but to Sasan it all seemed like a dream. But it was not.

Her people were down there in the village, locked in their own houses. Slowly she looked over at her brother and said, "You heard what the leader of the soldiers said. Our people are prisoners. We can do nothing by ourselves. It is too dangerous. We must get help." When he said nothing, she went on, "We must go to the Navy men at Kiska."

As they turned and began walking toward camp, Sasan felt a fresh wind on her face. She looked out over the cliffs to the sea and saw low clouds moving in towards the island. "Look," she said as she pointed, "the stormy weather comes, but it comes too late."

A NEW PROBLEM

Soon after Sasan crawled into her grass bed, she fell into a deep sleep. But not for long. The light of dawn and the sound of the wind made her eyes open. She had slept only a few short hours, but now lay wide awake. For a while she listened to the wind throwing itself against the rock shelter. The warmth of her bed and the safety of the shelter felt good as she slowly turned over in her mind all that had happened last night. Then her thoughts turned to what they must do during the coming day.

At last she stretched, crawled out, then shook her

brother. "Wake up," she called out, "We must go."

Sidak opened his eyes, then just as quickly closed them again. Sasan could not help thinking of Grandmother and how she would scold when he did that. But this morning Sasan did not feel like scolding him. He was so young and so much had happened to him in these last two days. She let him sleep and made ready to leave for Sarana Bay.

Sasan soon had everything back in their packs except for the raincoats. She put hers on and stepped out from behind the rock shelter to look around. The wind whipped a light rain against her face and she reached up to tie the hood of her raincoat tightly around her head. Wisps of clouds mixed with fog hung in the air and were driven along by the wind blowing in from the sea. As she stood there, warm and dry and with the wind full in her face, she was filled with a feeling of pride. Storms such as this had made the people of this island strong and unafraid. She was a part of both the island and its people. Last night she had feared the enemy soldiers; now she did not. And when she and her brother were out at sea, she would fear neither the storm nor the enemy. With that thought to strengthen her, she turned and went to wake her brother.

When Sidak was up at last, Sasan brought out the fish she had fried the night before. As they ate, she said, "When we get to Sarana Bay, you can clean more fish and cut them up for me to cook. While I am doing that, you must fill the water bags and check the other things we will need."

Sidak asked, "When will we leave for Kiska?"

"Tonight," she answered, "if we have everything ready, and it is not too stormy."

"But what if enemy soldiers come to our camp looking for the spy while we are there?" he asked.

Sasan answered, "We will do our work away from camp. If soldiers come, we will hide in one of the old houses up on the hill."

They finished the fish and set off at once. Sidak knew the way and walked in front as they headed down the hillside toward the creek that would lead them to Lost Lake. From there they would go through a low pass and on to Sarana Bay. Sasan was happy to see her brother so eager to carry out the new plan. Even with his heavy pack, he hurried along in front of her, and often she found it hard to keep up. When they came through the pass, Sidak wanted to keep on going, but Sasan insisted that they stop to rest.

The wind kept blowing in strong gusts and

whipped the grass about as it passed over the ground. Low clouds and fog, swept along by the wind, covered the pass where Sasan and her brother sat resting and hid Sarana Bay and their camp from view. Sidak asked, "Will it be too stormy for us to leave tonight?"

Sasan answered, "Grandmother and the older men have taught me how to travel across the sea when the sun and stars are hidden. But to do this one must begin the voyage in good weather in order to read the moving waters and set the course."

"I am tired of hiding from the enemy." He said this with growing anger in his voice. "I wish we could leave tonight."

"If we are ready by tonight, we can go as far as Shemya and wait for the storm to pass," Sasan answered. "No one lives on the island, we will not have to hide there. Then the next day we can go on to Kiska."

Sidak stood and picked up his pack. Sasan wanted to rest longer but she put hers on too and started down the mountain after him. Her tiredness left her when they came to some steep bluffs. There she heard the thunder of waves throwing themselves against the rocks below. This was the north end of Sarana Bay. Now only a few miles of sandy beach lay between them and the summer camp.

The steep climb down to the beach was slow and hard. When they were there at last, Sasan would not go on without resting again. While she sat, Sidak took off his pack, too, but would not rest. She watched him move back and forth at the water's edge then disappear into the fog toward the rocky beach at the bottom of the bluff. A moment later she heard his voice above the sound of the crashing waves. Quickly she ran in that direction.

This part of the beach was sheltered from the wind, but in the rain and fog she could not see more than a few feet ahead. Sidak was on his knees and bending over something when at last she spotted his light raincoat outlined against the dark rocks. "What is it?" she asked.

Sidak did not answer. But when Sasan stood next to him, she saw for herself why he had called. There against a rock, with his eyes closed and his face turned towards her, lay an enemy soldier. As she dropped to her knees, she asked, "Is he alive?"

"He does not seem to be," Sidak answered.

Sasan moved in closer and started unbuttoning the front of his uniform. It was soaked and felt cold to her touch. When her fingers reached through and touched the skin over his heart, it felt cold too. She held her hand still for a moment. As she did, her eyes fell on the soldier's face. He looked even younger than the two she had seen on the trail yesterday. Then her fingers picked up a faint heartbeat, and she said, "He is alive."

Sidak said, "We must leave at once."

"We cannot leave him here. If he is not taken to a warm, dry place he will die."

Sidak spoke now in an angry whisper, "Other enemy soldiers will come looking for him. Let them take care of him."

Sasan did not answer. Her hands were now busy searching over the soldier's head and the rest of his body. His hands were torn and bleeding, a long, deep cut caked with blood ran across the back of his neck, and his arms and legs were covered with small cuts and bruises. When she had finished, she said, more to herself than to her brother, "He has lost so much blood and is also weak from the wetness and the cold, but he has no broken bones."

Sidak looked around, then whispered, "We must go now. There are sure to be other enemy soldiers near."

"No," she said, "he has been out here for a long time. If he had been with other soldiers, he could have called out to them."

Anger once more returned to her brother's voice as he said, "You, yourself, have said he is not hurt badly."

"But he is too weak to help himself. If he is not cared for soon, he will die."

"Then he will die," Sidak whispered back. "You know we must help our people. How can we do that if we help the soldier? He will then know about us and will tell the others."

Even before her brother had spoken these words, Sasan's heart and mind were already struggling over what she should do. Because there had never been a doctor on the island, Grandmother had used the Old Ways to care for those who were hurt or sick. And Grandmother had taught Sasan much that she knew. Her mind knew exactly what should be done to save the soldier's life, and her heart urged her to do it. But her heart also urged her to think of her people in their time of need.

Sidak was now waiting for her answer. He became even more angry as he waited. At last he shouted down at her, "He is the enemy. He has come to take our island from us and to harm our people."

Sasan stood up slowly and turned toward her brother. The light rain that covered her face could not hide the tears in her eyes as she said, "Grandmother always said that both our church and the Old Ways tell us to love our enemies."

Sidak's anger pushed him to answer quickly, "Grandmother would also tell us to love our own people. Today we cannot do both."

Sasan answered firmly, "We must find a way to do both. But we must show our love for this soldier first, or he will die." She paused a moment, then added, "We must take him to our summer camp where he will be warm and dry."

Sidak still would not give in. "Just this morning you said we were not to use our summer house. You said the enemy might come and find us there."

"It is true," she answered, "we must not use it. But we can still use one of the old ones on the hill as we planned. It will be easy to carry our little stove and some dry grass up there. The stove will give us warmth as I cook the fish we need for our voyage."

Both stood looking at each other as the raindrops bounced off their raincoats and off their wet, shiny faces. Sasan's troubled face spoke louder than her words. "Can you think of a way to move him? He is too heavy for us to carry all the way to the summer camp."

Sidak answered simply, "We can use the bidarki."

His answer took a great worry from Sasan, and her mind turned quickly to other things that needed to be done. "I will go with you to get the boat. But first we must move the soldier to a drier place and try to cover him."

Together they pulled the soldier's limp body up on the grassy bank next to the beach. As soon as this was done, Sasan began taking off her raincoat and said, "Quickly, help me pull up some of the dead grass. I will put the raincoat over him to keep the rain off, then we will cover him with the grass to keep him warm."

This was soon done. Then, leaving their packs behind, they set off along the beach. When they came near their camp, Sasan thought once more of soldiers being there. She motioned to her brother, and they left the beach to walk along the grassy bank. Here they would leave no tracks, and they could hide in the grass if they had to.

As they came nearer, Sasan slowed her walking. After a while, she stopped to look around and to listen. The sounds of the waves crashing against the bluffs no longer came to her ears. A light breeze was coming from off the bay, but there was a stillness in the air around her. The heavy fog hid everything. She moved ahead slowly, her eyes searching for the barabaras at the summer camp which could not be too far off.

A little farther on she saw the dark shapes she was looking for. She touched her brother's arm, and together they started crawling through the grass. Every few minutes they stopped to listen for human sounds. When they reached the houses, they both stood for a moment looking and listening again for signs of soldiers. Satisfied there was no one in camp, they went straight to their own house and started moving things up the hill.

Most of the old houses up from camp had caved in over the years. But Sasan quickly found one that she had played in when she was a little girl. Its roof and walls still kept out the rain and wind. Carefully she pushed the old, dead grass aside and crawled through the opening where the door had been. Sidak, carrying the little cookstove and the stovepipe, crawled in behind her.

The room was small, and there was hardly enough light coming through the opening to see by. But it was dry inside and the place was well hidden. Sasan said, "Sidak, go back down to the shed and bring some dry driftwood and crowberry branches for the stove. While you do that, I will bring in the things we hid under the boat and make everything ready here."

Sidak started to crawl back out, and she reminded him, "Make sure we have left no signs."

It took only a few minutes to do all this, and not long after they were both seated in the boat, headed for the bluffs. For a moment, Sasan felt strange paddling in the rain without her raincoat. But then her mind turned quickly to the problem to which she still had no answer.

With both of them paddling, the boat skimmed across the swells close to the shore. In a short time they were again on the beach next to the bluffs. The soldier still lay just where they had left him. Sasan took a moment to feel his heartbeat again and was gladdened when she found it stronger. Then they uncovered him and carried him over next to the boat. Sasan went back to get her raincoat. When she returned, Sidak said, "We can lay him between the two holes, but we cannot keep our balance with him riding there."

"Then what will we do?" she asked.

Sidak started taking off his shoes as he answered, "We will both walk along in the shallow water next to

the beach. That way we can push the boat and balance it with our hands."

Sasan could not help feeling proud of her brother
for his helpful ideas. She was also pleased that he
seemed no longer angry at her for helping the soldier. Sidak saw her standing there trying to speak and
said, "Hurry, take off your shoes and put them in the
boat."

Soon they were walking along in the water with the
soldier and their packs riding on the boat. When they
came to the beach near the camp, Sasan stopped to
listen. Then, moving slowly, she turned the bow
toward deeper water. Like shadows they moved past
the camp. When she heard the waters of the creek
running over the fish dam, she pulled the boat back
in toward shore. They landed it on a rocky stretch of
beach next to the creek and began carrying the sol-

dier up the hill. He was heavy, and they had to put him down often to rest. Once while they did this Sasan checked the soldier's heartbeat and found it weaker—much as it was when they first found him.

"Quick," she said, "we must get him to the shelter. His body grows weaker and must be made warm soon, or he will die."

When at last they had him inside, both of them struggled to get off his shoes and wet uniform. Sasan found an old raincoat in the pile of extra things, and they slipped this on him. Then they covered him over with dry grass. As soon as they had finished, Sasan said, "Sidak, you must go and carry the boat back to its hiding place and bring the packs. I will set up the stove and start a fire."

The warmth of the fire soon filled the small room and Sasan felt better. The soldier was safe and dry. Cleaning his cuts would have to wait until water could be heated. Then, when he awoke, she would give him some herb tea. She leaned back against the dirt wall, closed her eyes, and rested.

THE SOLDIER

Sasan sat for a long while with her eyes closed. Slowly the warmth of the fire began creeping through her wet clothes and into her tired body. She heard her brother come in and put the packs on the floor, then crawl over to where she sat. But she did not open her eyes or speak to him.

After some of the numbness had left Sasan's body, her mind turned back to the thing that worried her. She reached over and laid her hand on the soldier's head. Warmth was slowly returning to his body. She looked over at her brother and said, "He will live."

These words seemed to bring Sidak out of his silence. He asked, "When he is strong once more and awakens, what will we do with him then?"

"If we quickly make ready the food and water, perhaps we can leave before he is strong enough to stop us."

Sidak was not satisfied with her answer. He went on, "In this storm? Did you not say we needed good weather to begin the voyage?"

Sasan nodded her head. "Yes," she answered, "but I told you, we could go over to Shemya. We would be safe there."

"Would we?" he asked. "How long do you think it would take him to reach the village and tell his leader about us?" Without waiting for an answer he went on, "Shemya is the first place they would go to look for us. Remember, large boats brought the soldiers to our island. They will use these to search for us. They will never let us reach Kiska."

Sasan said, "The sea is wide and our boat is small. It will not be easy for them to find us."

Sidak sat thinking for a moment, then said, "This time I will do as you ask. I will start by going now to clean the fish."

As he spoke, he began crawling toward the opening. When he reached it, he turned and said, "I will not be here to protect you with my knife if he should awaken. We must tie his hands and feet now so you will be safe."

"But, Sidak," Sasan said with surprise in her voice, "he has lost blood. He has suffered much from being in the rain and the cold so long. He will still be weak when he awakens."

Sidak crawled back over to where she sat. He looked into her eyes, and Sasan saw the flash of anger on his face. "I helped you save the soldier's life because that was your wish. Now it is my wish that he be tied. He is the enemy, and he will do all he can to keep us from getting help for our people. He will even kill us if he has to."

Sasan tried to make him understand. "You are right. He is a soldier, and he must do all he can to help his people win. But surely you do not think he will be able to harm me when he is still so weak? Can we not wait a little longer before we tie him up?"

Sidak still stared at her in anger. "You think because I am younger than you that I do not know what is right. But I do."

This time Sasan agreed, "It will be done as you wish. Help me, so you can then go clean the fish."

Sidak took cord from his pack and after they finished and her brother had left, Sasan put her hand once more on the soldier's head. His skin no longer felt cold to her touch. She was almost sure she could feel his breathing. "He will be waking soon," she thought, "and what will he think when he finds his hands and feet tied?"

She looked long into his boyish face, then pulled her hand away and crawled over to check the stove. "Why did the war have to come here?" she asked, but she knew there could be no answer.

Suddenly Sasan's mood changed, and she started doing things. First she put more wood on the fire and put water on to heat, then she crawled outside and looked at the stovepipe to see if there was smoke. Seeing that there was none, she looked around at the weather. The fog was still thick. It and the rain kept her from seeing the camp just below. The winds had grown stronger. The new grass growing over the old houses waved wildly as the wind swept over it. She listened for sounds other than the wind, but heard none. Sasan felt sure at last that their hiding place was safe from the eyes of anyone who might come searching for the soldier.

Just as she was going to crawl back into the warm,

dry shelter, her brother appeared out of the fog carrying a board piled high with strips of fish ready to cook. "I brought these so you can get started," he said.

Sidak gave her the fish and had turned to go back when she reminded him, "Remember, soldiers might come to search our camp and the beach. Listen carefully as you work and leave no signs."

Sidak nodded to show he understood, then turned and disappeared again into the fog. Sasan took the fish strips inside and started putting them on top of the stove.

While sitting and watching the fish cook, she heard a slight sound behind her. Turning quickly, she saw that the soldier was lying on his side. His eyes were open, and he was staring at her. His hands, tied together in front of him, were sticking out from underneath the grass that covered the rest of his body.

He kept staring and Sasan stared back. She did not know what else to do. Ever since they found him, the soldier had been almost without life. His eyes had stayed closed, he had not moved, and he had not said a word. Now, as if a miracle had happened, the soldier was alive again and Sasan did not know how to act towards him. She felt a need to talk to him; to tell him that she was glad he was alive and feeling better. But she could not do this because he did not speak her language. And even more important, because he was her enemy. He was one of those who had come to capture this island and take away the freedom of its people.

Sasan could not think of anything else to do, so she turned back to the stove and started moving the strips of fish. As she kept herself busy with this, she remembered Grandmother's reminder that she love everyone, even her enemies. Then, it had seemed like such an easy thing to do. It seemed easy because back then she had no enemies. Now it was different.

Sasan was still struggling with this problem when she was surprised by the soldier's voice. It filled the small room with its sound. She could hardly believe her ears as he asked in English, "Who are you? And where am I?"

She turned once more and sat facing him. But now without thinking, she answered, "I am Sasan. My brother and I found you lying on the beach and brought you here."

Somehow as soon as she said these words, Sasan knew how she would act toward this soldier. Even though he was her enemy, she must treat him with kindness and care for him just as she had done when they had first found him. Treating him with kindness need not keep her from making the voyage and helping her people become free once more.

For a moment she forgot the fish on the stove and crawled over closer to him. "You are still weak and should rest. You will be safe here," she said.

The soldier answered, "But I do not understand. Did you escape from your village? Why are you helping me?"

Sasan did not want to answer his first question and did not know how to answer the second. So she moved back to the stove and to her work.

There was silence for a moment, then Sasan was again surprised when she heard him use her name. "Sasan," he said, "you do not have to answer. I know all that I need to know. I know that you saved my life even though I am an enemy soldier."

Sasan turned to him and asked, "Are you well enough to eat?"

He nodded, and she took a piece of the cooked fish over to where he lay. Since his hands were tied, he had to reach out with both of them to take the fish from her fork. Sasan saw this and asked, "Do you not wonder why your hands and feet are tied?"

The soldier answered, "I do not wonder. I understand why you must do this." After a moment, he said, "Sasan, I am glad you tied my hands and feet."

Surprised, she asked, "But why?"

"I am a soldier," he answered, "if I were not tied, I would have to try to escape."

Just as he finished these words, Sidak struggled through an opening with another pile of fish strips. He placed these by the stove. Then he looked from the soldier over to Sasan. After a few moments of silence the soldier spoke. "You are Sasan's brother. I am Taro. You and your sister have saved my life. I wish there was some way I could repay you for your kindness."

Sidak answered coldly, "We will be repaid when you and the other soldiers free our people and leave this island."

Taro heard this unfriendliness and said, "If I were you, I, too, would be angry."

Again there was silence. Without looking at her brother, Sasan knew his anger had now turned to an open hate and that Taro's friendly words would only add to this hate. To make things easier, she asked, "What happened to you last night?"

Taro seemed glad to have a chance to explain. He answered, "When I finished my turn at guard, I could not sleep and went for a walk. It was a beautiful night, and my thoughts took me back to my home and my family. I forgot everything else. When I looked around at last, I was lost."

Sasan asked, "Had the storm already struck? Is that why you could not see the searchlight in the village?"

"No," Taro answered, "it was still clear when I stopped to look around. I did look for the light, but it could not be seen. I became afraid and started to run. Then the storm struck, and I hurried even more. As I ran my fear grew stronger, until at last it pushed everything else from my mind. I do not remember coming to the beach where you found me. I must have fallen but I remember nothing."

None of the unfriendliness had left Sidak's voice as he said, "There are no trees on this island. Even without the moon's light you should have been able to climb up one of the peaks and look for the light in the village from there."

Taro could only answer, "It is easy for you to think of those things. You have learned how to find your way across wild places. I have lived all my life in a big city."

Sasan suddenly wanted to know more about Taro. She asked, "Have you never been away from your home before?"

"Never," Taro answered, "and I miss my father, and my mother, and my sister very much." He paused, then added, "It is hard for one like me to be a soldier."

Now Sasan felt even closer to Taro. She wanted to know more about his family. But instead she asked, "Where did you learn English?"

"Our schools teach it. I learned it so I could write to one of my cousins who lives in your country, in a placed called California."

Sidak put an end to the questions by saying, "Sasan, while we sit here listening to this enemy soldier, we give his friends more time in which to find us and keep us from leaving."

Sasan wished he had not spoken. Now Taro knew of their plan to leave the island. She saw that he, too, had not meant to speak of it. "Sidak," she said, "you are right. Soldiers will come looking for Taro, and we must make sure they do not find our hiding place. Go outside to watch, and I will come out as soon as I have put more fish on the stove."

Sidak left and Sasan went about her work. When she finished, she put on her raincoat. As she was going out, she said to Taro, "We will be outside. Try to rest again."

When Sasan crawled outdoors, a cold rain hit her face. Fog still hung over the hillside, but the wind had stopped, and in the still evening air she could again hear the far-away booming of the waves against the bluff. Her brother sat huddled in his raincoat next to the old house that stood in front of theirs. Quietly she walked over and sat down next to him.

"Have you heard any sounds in the camp?" she asked.

"Nothing," he answered.

Then she asked, "Are you angry because I treat the soldier with kindness?"

He shrugged his shoulders. She went on, "If hating

Taro would help us free our people, I would hate him, too. But it will not. There is much for us to do. We must put all our time and strength into our work."

Sidak turned to her and asked, "Can we go over to Shemya now?"

Sasan answered, "I cooked much of the fish while we talked. You could fill the water bag while I put some fishing line and other things we might need into one of the packs."

Sidak started to get up, but Sasan put her hand on his arm. "But wait," she said, "we must first decide what to do about Taro."

"We will leave him here," Sidak said.

"Tied up?"

"Yes," he answered angrily, "otherwise he would capture us and take us back to the village. We could not stop him."

"But he would die if we leave him here!" Sasan exclaimed.

"Soldiers will come to the camp looking for him. He can crawl to the door and call out to them."

Her brother's idea seemed like a good one, and a feeling of happiness came over her. But just for a moment. "We cannot leave him," she heard herself saying.

"Why not?" asked Sidak.

"The soldiers might come at any moment," she answered. "Certainly they will be here before the night is over."

Sasan paused and then Sidak spoke, "Yes, and just now the soldier heard me tell about our plan to leave the island. He will tell them, and then their boats will come looking for us."

Often before Sasan had sat like this, warm and comfortable, listening to the patter of rain on her coat and feeling rain against her face. This and the smell of the sea and the silence all around her had always brought peace and a quiet happiness. Now she smelled the same sea air, heard and felt the same rain, but it brought only sadness.

At last Sidak broke the stillness, "Perhaps you could go in and make the soldier believe we are only leaving for another part of the island. That we plan to hide there. He trusts you and will believe what you tell him. Then when he tells the other soldiers, they will look for us on the island. But we will be safely on our way to Kiska."

Sasan did not have time to answer Sidak. Just then she heard a call. The sound came from far up the trail, toward the village. It seemed to be carried slowly up the hillside by the fog itself. She listened and heard another. This one seemed closer. Then a third call. Sasan heard it clearly: "Ta-r-oo."

Sidak whispered, "They are calling his name. They are searching for him and coming this way."

THE THIRD NIGHT

As Sasan crawled through the door, her thoughts were on Taro. From the darkness at the back of the barabara she heard him ask, "Is this place well hidden?"

Before she could answer, Sidak said, "They will not find us here unless you call out to them."

Taro answered quietly, "I will not do that."

Sidak was now next to Sasan. In the faint light coming through the doorway she saw him draw the knife from his belt. "I will make sure you do not," he said.

"This knife you see in my hand will stop you if you try."

Taro's voice was firm and without fear. He said, "I will not call out. But it will not be because of your knife."

Sasan believed Taro, but she knew Sidak did not. A plan had come to her while she listened, and she said, "Sidak, we cannot stay here and guard Taro when the soldiers are searching the camp."

"But why not? This is a good place to hide."

Sasan answered, "If they search the hillside, we will be trapped here."

"Where else could we hide?" he asked.

"We can put the food and our other things in our packs, then wait outside as they search the camp. If we hear anyone coming up the hillside, we will slip away in the fog." Sasan paused, then went on slowly and clearly so that Taro would be sure to hear, "We will find some other place on the island to hide."

Without waiting for Sidak to say anything, Sasan turned toward Taro and said, "You have told me yourself that you are a soldier and must try to escape. I will tie my scarf over your mouth before we go outside. Then if the soldiers do come and find you, they will know why you did not call out for help."

Sasan carefully, but gently, placed the scarf across his mouth making sure it was well between his teeth so it could not be pushed away. Then she tied it firmly around his head, and said, "We will also have to tie your hands behind your back so you cannot pull the scarf away."

Sasan and Sidak were soon finished with the tying and the packing. While her brother carried the packs outside, Sasan took a moment to make Taro comfortable. As she finished, she whispered, "I am sorry." Then she slipped quietly out the doorway.

It was dark when Sasan came and stood next to her brother. She listened for just a moment. The soldiers were already in the camp and the voices were now moving along the beach. She whispered, "Bring your pack and follow me."

Sidak whispered back, "Where are we going?"

Sasan answered, "It is too late to escape but we will move the boat to the other side of the hill. If we hear the soldiers coming too near, we will try to get it down to the beach and into the water without being seen, then cross over to Shemya. But Taro will think we went to hide somewhere on the island."

After they carried the boat down the other side of the hill, they left their packs alongside it and crawled back up to their hiding place. The voices in the camp came up to them through the fog.

A little later Sasan heard talk and footsteps along the beach near the mouth of the creek. She held her breath and grabbed her brother's arm. One of the voices seemed to be moving towards their hiding place. The voice grew louder, and she tugged at his arm. Together they began crawling away through the grass. Then she stopped one last time and heard a call from farther up the beach. After that the voices and footsteps moved away, and she knew they were safe for a short while at least.

Sasan listened for just a moment longer to make sure none of the soldiers had stayed behind. Then she and Sidak crawled back to where they had been before. Again they sat and listened, ready to slip off down the hillside if anyone came near. Sasan could now hear soldiers calling Taro's name all along the beach, both above and below the camp.

After what seemed like hours of waiting, Sasan heard someone near the camp blow a whistle. Then there was the sound of many voices and footsteps hurrying towards the camp. All at once the voices and footsteps stopped. For a moment all Sasan could hear was the pounding of her heart. She waited and listened.

"Should they try to escape before it was too late?"

Then suddenly, it was all over. One of the soldiers shouted. This was followed by the sound of more footsteps as the soldiers marched away into the night. They were marching back along the trail to the village.

Sasan and Sidak sat until the sound of the footsteps no longer could be heard and the camp below was quiet once more. Somehow the stillness, the fog, and the smell of the sea had never seemed so good.

But this mood did not last long. Other thoughts cut short Sasan's joy. They must leave for Shemya as soon as possible, but she still did not know what to do about Taro.

At last she turned to Sidak and said, "We must leave for Shemya now."

Sidak had been waiting long to hear her say this. He answered, "Everything will be ready after I fill the water bag at the creek."

He got up to go, but Sasan pulled him back down. "Wait," she said, "we still have not decided what to do about Taro."

Sidak asked in surprise, "Did we not decide to leave him tied?"

"Yes," answered Sasan, "we decided that when we

thought the soldiers were coming, and they would then free him. Now the soldiers have already come and gone. If we go now and leave him tied, he will not be found. He will die."

"We cannot untie him before we go," Sidak argued. "You know he will have to capture us."

"We do not know that," Sasan answered calmly. "If he promises not to, he will keep his word."

"But he himself told you he is a soldier," Sidak said. "That he must help his people by trying to escape. If he must do that, he must also try to capture us."

Sasan had thought of this, too, but she had no answer. She could only say, "Remember, he is grateful to us for saving his life. He has told us he wants to repay our kindness."

Sidak's voice grew louder as his anger increased. He asked, "Do you really believe he would have kept his word? That he would not have called out to the soldiers if we had not put the scarf in his mouth?"

Sasan answered firmly, "Yes, I do. I put the scarf in his mouth in case the soldiers found him. So they would know that he was not trying to help us."

For a time no word passed between them. Sidak was filled with anger towards his sister, and she felt only doubt and unhappiness.

Then suddenly Sasan heard a voice in the darkness behind her. Without thinking she turned to face it. She froze for a moment. Then she heard the voice say, "Sasan," and she knew it was Taro. "I did not mean to frighten you. I wanted you to know that you did right in trusting me."

By this time the terror had left Sasan, but she was still confused. "What do you mean?" she asked. "I don't understand. How did you get untied?"

She could not see Taro, but in the darkness next to her, she saw her brother's hand move towards his knife. She grabbed his arm as Taro laughed and said, "Do not worry. I am not untied. But I did get the scarf out of my mouth soon after you and Sidak left."

"How did you do it?" she asked.

Taro answered, "A piece of wood was sticking out of the earth wall near me. By pushing my cheek up against it I was able to hook the scarf and pull it away from my mouth."

By this time Sasan and Sidak had left their hiding place in the tall grass next to the barabara and could see Taro lying on his side in the doorway. His hands were still tied behind his back. His head was on the ground, and he turned his face trying to look up at her.

Sasan wanted to help him, but she stood there staring. At last she asked, "Why did you not call out for help when the soldiers were so near?"

Taro answered quietly, "Because I promised you I would not."

Sasan saw rain falling on his face and said to her brother. "Help me move him back inside where he will be dry."

With Taro helping, they soon made him comfortable against the wall next to the stove. Sasan then opened the stove door and put some crowberry branches on the coals. The branches burst into flame and Sasan left the stove door open so they would have a little light to see by.

When all this was finished, Taro said, "After the soldiers left, I rolled myself over to the doorway." He paused for just a moment, then added, "I heard you and Sidak talking."

"Then you know of our plans?"

"Yes," Taro answered, "you will take your boat and leave this island." He waited for them to speak. When they did not, he went on, "If you free me before you leave, I promise not to capture you."

Sidak spoke now. Sasan was glad there was no anger in his voice. "Why should you keep such a promise?" You have repaid us once for saving your life. You owe us nothing more."

Taro answered, "I will keep this promise to repay your sister's trust in me." He paused, then went on, "Sidak, you did not trust me in the beginning, and I do not blame you for this. But now I think I have earned your trust."

Sidak said nothing for a moment. The light from the fire fell on his face as he sat with his head down thinking. At last Sasan saw him slowly draw the knife from his belt and hand it to her. She took the knife, then kneeled down and cut away the cords that bound Taro's feet. Next she cut away those from his hands, and he was free.

Not long after Taro was freed, the boat lay on the beach loaded and ready. It was time to leave. A strange feeling of emptiness came over Sasan. So much had happened in these past few days, and now she was leaving this island of her people.

She watched Taro turn to her brother and put out his hand. Sidak paused for a moment as if in doubt. Seeing this, Taro said, "I am sorry this war has made me your enemy."

After hearing these words, Sidak took Taro's hand and shook it. For a moment their eyes met. Then Sidak turned and made ready to enter the boat.

Now it was Sasan's turn to say goodbye to this stranger who was also her enemy. The lazy lapping water washed against the sand but Sasan did not hear it. Nor did she feel the light rain fall against her face. She was trying so hard to say something to tell Taro how she felt. But the words would not come.

Instead, it was he who spoke. "Your kindness and your trust must be rewarded. I know it is wrong, but just this once I will not carry out my duty as a soldier. I will tell no one about you."

Sasan answered, "In this war we do what we must do and the Old Ways tell us we must love even our enemy." With these words, she turned toward the waiting boat.

It took her but a moment to tie the raincoat around the hole. Then without looking back she jabbed her paddle into the water and felt the boat slide away from the beach. She turned the bow to the northeast, towards Shemya. She noted carefully how the boat cut across the swells. These swells would be her only guide once they left the shore and could no longer hear the waves washing against it.

When Sasan had taken care of all this, she glanced quickly towards the beach. It had already disappeared into the night. But she heard Taro's voice carry across the water and through the fog. "Goodbye, Sidak." he said. "Goodbye Sasan. Tonight may your God hold you in the palm of his hand." Then there was stillness again, except for the lapping of water against the sides of the boat as the paddles sped it towards Shemya.

Time passed quickly for Sasan. She paddled, but her eyes were always on the water; using its movement to give her direction.

It seemed only a short time later when she heard the familiar sound of waves washing against the shore. She called out to her brother, "It is Shemya, but we will stay offshore and paddle to the eastern side. It has a good beach, and we can rest there before leaving on the long voyage to Kiska."

It was dark and there was still much fog, but Sasan knew her brother must be smiling as he turned and said, "I could sleep well tonight even on a bed of rocks."

It was not long before they swung around to the eastern side of the island and then brought their boat to rest on a sandy beach.

Moments later they were walking among the big rocks next to the beach looking for a sheltered place. Suddenly Sasan sensed someone behind her. She thought she heard Sidak stumble. But before she could turn, she felt something come across her throat and cut off her breath. That was all she remembered.

When Sasan awoke, she lay with her eyes closed, trying to remember. Without opening her eyes she knew this was a strange place. She was lying on something soft. Even with no raincoat or jacket on, she felt warm and dry. All around her the air was filled with a quiet hum; one that she had never heard before.

Sasan was afraid to open her eyes, afraid she would see enemy soldiers all around her. But at last she did open them. The room she was in seemed empty at first. It was warm and dry here, but everything looked so strange. A smell filled the air, a smell that reminded her of the ship that came each year to their island, and the ceiling over her head was so close; she felt she could reach up and touch it. Except for a low hum, everything was quiet. Slowly she turned her head to one side. Then she saw it. The thing that filled her with dread. Sitting at a table, with his back to her, was a man in a brown uniform. The enemy had captured them at last. For a long while she lay there staring at the back of the man's head. The hope that had always been with her and had given her strength was now gone. She turned her head away and closed her eyes once more.

Then someone asked, "Are you awake?" and her hope returned. Quickly she turned her head and opened her eyes. The man was smiling at her. "You are safe," he said. "This is an American submarine."

For a moment Sasan did not know what to think or what to say. The man went on, "Tonight we landed scouts on Shemya to see if there were Japanese soldiers there. It was so dark and stormy when you landed, they thought you were enemy soldiers. So they captured you and brought you back to the submarine."

Sasan asked, "My brother, is he safe?"

"Yes, he is here, too," the man answered. "He has already told us about your people, and we have sent a message for help."

Sasan sat up and looked around. The man said, "If

you feel well enough, I will take you to him now."

"Where is he?" she asked.

"He was hungry," the man answered with a smile. "The cook is feeding him in the next room. Perhaps you are hungry, too?"

Sasan smiled and nodded her head. He opened the door for her, and said, "After you eat, you both must rest. And after you have rested, we will ask for your help. You can tell us much that we need to know about your island and about the enemy soldiers there." Then he closed the door and left her.

Sasan went in and sat down across from her brother. He stopped eating. For a moment they sat looking at each other. He was tired, but she saw only the happiness in his face.

"Remember," she said, "there is still much to do."

"Yes," he answered, "we did our job. Now the American soldiers know. They will help us."

All was quiet again. Then, slowly a smile spread over Sasan's face, and she said, "Troubles are like the wind, they do not go on forever. And so we must always remember what Grandmother told us: the wind is not a river."

ABOUT THE AUTHOR

Arnold Griese taught for several years in a one-room school in an Athabaskan village in the Alaskan interior. His experiences and travels in that area, and his love for the Alaskan people and their tales of ancient days, inspired his first two books for children, *At the Mouth of the Luckiest River* and *The Way of Our People*.

During the long Alaskan winter evenings, he would read about places like the tiny Aleutian island of Attu, and, in 1976, he received permission from the Coast Guard to spend a month backpacking and camping on the island. There, with only a decayed Japanese vessel and a bronze plaque to remind him of the village of the past, he began writing *The Wind Is Not a River.*

Mr. Griese grew up on a farm in Iowa, one of a large family to whom reading was always important. At seventeen he left the farm to find his fortune. His travels took him through most of the western states and to Hawaii and Mexico. After service in World War II, he was graduated from Georgetown University and earned his master's degree at the University of Miami and his doctorate at the University of Arizona. He went on to join the faculty of the University of Alaska as professor of children's literature. Mr. Griese is also the author of *Anna's Athabaskan Summer.* He lives in Fairbanks, Alaska.

ABOUT THE ILLUSTRATOR

Shortly after her graduation from Abilene Christian College, Glo Coalson went to Alaska, where her brother Douglas was working with Eskimo reindeer herders in a Bureau of Indian Affairs program. For almost ten months she lived with her brother and sister-in-law in Kotzebue, the largest Eskimo village, which is just above the Arctic Circle. While she was there, she made many drawings of Eskimo life, which were later exhibited at the Anchorage Historical and Fine Arts Museum. She left Alaska and moved to New

York City, where she launched her career as an illustrator. Among Ms. Coalson's many books are *On Mother's Lap* by Ann Herbert Scott and *At the Mouth of the Luckiest River* by Arnold Griese. She now makes her home in Dallas, Texas.